RETURN OF THE JEDI

A STORYBOOK BY
J.J. GARDNER

ADAPTED FROM THE SCREENPLAY BY
LAWRENCE KASDAN AND GEORGE LUCAS

STORY BY
GEORGE LUCAS

SCHOLASTIC INC.
NEW YORK   TORONTO   LONDON   AUCKLAND   SYDNEY

No part of this publication may be reproduced in whole or in part, or stored in a retrieval system, or transmitted in any form or by any means, electronic, mechanical, photocopying, recording, or otherwise, without written permission of the publisher. For information regarding permission, write to Scholastic Inc., 555 Broadway, New York, NY 10012.

ISBN 0-590-06659-5

™ & ® & © 1997 by Lucasfilm Ltd. All rights reserved.
Published by Scholastic Inc.

12 11 10 9 8 7 6 5 4 3 2 1   7 8 9/9 0 1 2/0

Designed by Joan Ferrigno
Edited by Allan Kausch (Lucasfilm) and Ellen Stamper (Scholastic)

Printed in the U.S.A.   14

First Scholastic printing, February 1997

A LONG TIME AGO IN A GALAXY FAR, FAR AWAY . . . .

The Galactic Empire has secretly begun construction on a new armored space station even more powerful than the first dreaded Death Star. When completed, this ultimate weapon will spell certain doom for the small band of Rebels struggling to restore freedom to the galaxy. . . .

Meanwhile, Luke Skywalker has returned to his home planet of Tatooine. In an attempt to rescue his friend Han Solo, he sent a message with his two droids, C-3PO and R2-D2, to the palace of the vile gangster Jabba the Hutt . . . .

"**R**₂, are you sure this is the right place?" asked C-3PO nervously. He and his little companion droid stood before the giant palace of Jabba the Hutt.

R2 let out a series of nervous beeps.

"Of course I'm worried," replied C-3PO. "And you should be, too. Lando Calrissian never returned from this awful place. Well, I better knock, I suppose."

And with that the tall golden droid timidly knocked on the great iron door of the palace.

"There doesn't seem to be anyone here," said C-3PO with a sigh of relief. "Let's go back and tell Master Luke."

But before the two droids could retreat, a small hatch in the middle of the door opened. A spidery mechanical arm with an electronic eyeball on the end popped out and inspected the visitors.

"Tee chuta hhat yudd!" demanded the mechanical sentry.

C-3PO responded by immediately identifying himself and R2. Satisfied, the sentry popped back into the hatch. No sooner had it disappeared than the great iron door of the palace screeched open. R2 started inside.

"R2, wait!" called C-3PO, following nervously. "I really don't think we should rush into all this."

But by then it was too late. First the great door to the palace slammed shut behind them. Then they were met by two giant green Gamorrean guards. The guards led the two frightened droids deeper into the palace. Suddenly, from out of the darkness emerged a slender-looking being with tentacles coming out of his head. He was Bib Fortuna, Jabba the Hutt's special assistant.

"We bring a message to your master, Jabba the Hutt," replied C-3PO when Bib Fortuna asked what the droids wanted.

R2 beeped a reply. "And a gift," translated C-3PO. Although he had no idea what the gift was.

Bib Fortuna held out his hand and awaited the gift, but R2 insisted on giving it only to Jabba himself. Bib sneered. Then he gestured for the droids to follow him deeper into the palace.

The droids followed Bib through several dark and smelly hallways until they reached a dimly lit chamber crowded with vile, grotesque creatures. In the center of the room, sitting on a throne, was the most wretched looking of all these creatures. It was Jabba the Hutt. He was a giant worm-like alien with skin that dripped with slime. His eyes were as wily looking as a snake's and his breath was as bad as the garbage chamber of a starship.

"*Bo Shuda!*" roared Jabba.

"Good morning," C-3PO replied, nervously shaking from head to toe. "The message, R2. The message." And with that R2 projected a beam of light from his domed head. Soon the light formed an image of Luke Skywalker.

"Greetings, Exalted One," the recorded image of Luke said to Jabba. "I am Luke Skywalker, Jedi Knight and friend to Captain Solo. I seek an audience with Your Greatness to bargain for Solo's life. As a token of my goodwill, I present you with a gift: these two droids. Both are hardworking and will serve you well."

C-3PO was startled by Luke's offer. "This can't be!" he exclaimed.

"There will be no bargain," said Jabba with a hideous laugh.

"We're doomed!" C-3PO gasped.

"I like Captain Solo where he is," Jabba continued. He glanced behind his throne. A slab of carbonite hung on the wall. Embedded in the carbonite was the frozen form of Han Solo. A terrified expression was fixed across his face. He had been this way since the evil Darth Vader had captured him back on Bespin.

It was decided that R2-D2 would serve on Jabba the Hutt's sail barge. Since C-3PO was a protocol droid and fluent in over six million forms of communication, he remained in the throne room as an interpreter for the evil crime lord.

C-3PO had been at his new post only a short time when an unnatural quiet swept over the rowdy crowd. All heads turned as two figures entered the room and marched straight up to Jabba the Hutt. C-3PO did not know the shorter figure, a bounty hunter whose face was hidden by an odd helmet. But he instantly recognized the bounty hunter's captive. It was Han Solo's copilot, Chewbacca the Wookiee.

"At last we have the mighty Chewbacca," said Jabba the Hutt in his own language.

"I have come for the bounty on this Wookiee," said the bounty hunter. "I want fifty thousand. No less."

Jabba laughed at the amount, wondering aloud why he should have to pay so much. Then the bounty hunter held up a small silver ball that began to glow in his hand. It was a thermal detonator, a bomb. Everyone cowered with fear. After some tense discussion, Jabba agreed to pay the bounty hunter for Chewbacca and ordered his guards to take the Wookiee away.

Later that night the bounty hunter sneaked back into Jabba's throne room. He carefully made his way to the carbonite slab containing Han Solo. He then flipped a switch on the side of the slab. This deactivated the force field around the slab and lowered it to the ground. Next, the bounty hunter slid the decarbonization lever to one side. Immediately, the slab began to hum. The shell surrounding Han began to melt away. The bounty hunter watched as Han slowly came to life.

"Just relax for a moment," the bounty hunter told Han. "You're free of the carbonite."

"Where am I?" asked Han groggily.

"Jabba's palace," replied the bounty hunter.

"Who are you?" asked Han.

The bounty hunter removed his helmet and revealed himself to be Princess Leia. "Someone who loves you," Leia told Han gently as she cradled him in her arms. "I gotta get you out of here."

But no sooner had Leia helped Han to his feet than a curtain slid open, revealing Jabba the Hutt and a group of criminals. They had been watching all along and were now hysterical with laughter. Then Jabba ordered his guards to take Han to Chewbacca's cell. As for Princess Leia, he had her placed in chains so he could keep her beside him as a slave.

It was an easy matter for Luke Skywalker to gain access to Jabba's palace. Once there, he skillfully used his Jedi mind powers to persuade Bib Fortuna to take him into the throne room and announce his arrival to the crime lord.

Then he tried to use the same powers on Jabba himself. "You will bring Captain Solo and the Wookiee to me," Luke commanded Jabba, staring hard at the slimy, giant worm.

"Your mind powers will not work on me, boy," Jabba said, laughing. "There will be no bargain, young Jedi. I shall enjoy watching you die."

And with that Jabba raised his hand, and the floor beneath Luke gave way. Luke plummeted into a dungeon-like pit below. He quickly looked around for an escape, but what he saw next made his heart skip a beat. A rancor, a giant creature with fangs and sharp claws, emerged from behind an iron gate.

The rancor started for Luke, swiping at the young Jedi with its huge claws. Luke darted out of the way and squeezed into a crevice in the pit wall. Then he grabbed a large rock and smashed it down on the monster's paw.

The rancor howled with pain, momentarily stunned. Luke dashed toward the iron gate that led to another room, but there was nowhere to hide. He was trapped and the rancor was again moving toward him, baring its huge, hungry fangs.

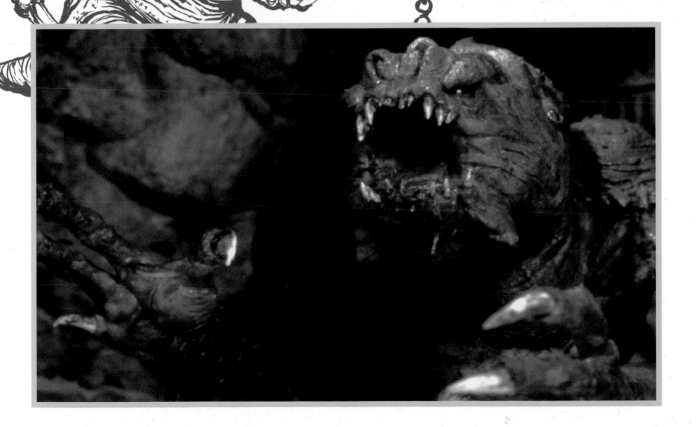

Just then Luke noticed a control panel next to the iron gate. Thinking quickly, he picked up a nearby skull and threw it at the buttons on the panel. The panel exploded. The iron gate came crashing down on the rancor's head, killing the beast.

Jabba was angry that Luke had killed his favorite pet. "Bring me Solo and the Wookiee," he commanded his guards. "They will all suffer for this outrage!"

As punishment, Luke, Han, and Chewbacca were taken into the desert on an anti-gravity skiff. There they hovered over the Great Pit of Carkoon. Inside the pit was the deadly Sarlacc, a creature that lived beneath the dunes. Jabba's guards led Luke to the edge of a gangplank and prepared to push him into the pit.

"Jabba!" Luke called out as he teetered at the edge of the plank. "Free us or die!"

Jabba was nearby, watching from his personal sail barge. He ignored Luke's threat, laughing hideously as his guards pushed Luke toward the end of the plank. Standing beside Jabba, R2-D2 let out a series of worried beeps.

But Luke had a plan. He glanced over to one of the masked guards and nodded. He knew the guard was none other than Lando Calrissian. Lando had been patiently awaiting Luke's signal.

Suddenly Luke felt himself being pushed over the edge of the plank by Jabba's guard. No sooner had Luke begun to fall than he grabbed the edge of the plank with his fingertips and catapulted himself skyward. In midair, he did a complete flip. Then he dropped back down onto the skiff and extended his hand. His lightsaber was now hurtling toward him, thrown to him by R2, who had cleverly sneaked it aboard Jabba's sail barge.

Luke ignited the sword. Then, with amazing speed, he sent overboard the monstrous guards who had prodded him off the plank. More guards came after him. One by one he fought them off with his lightsaber, working his way back on the skiff's deck as he went.

By now Lando had removed his mask and joined the fight. This gave Luke enough time to release Han and Chewbacca from their handcuffs.

At that moment a cannon blast from Jabba's barge rocked the skiff. Lando lost his balance and was tossed over the side of the shaking skiff. As he fell he grabbed a rope. But he was now dangling only a few short centimeters above the sand pit and the hungry Sarlacc.

"Help!" cried Lando.

Han ran to Lando's aid, a spear in his hand. He leaned over the deck and extended the spear. Lando, one hand clutching the rope, reached up and tried to grab the spear. Suddenly the rope broke and Lando fell.

Han extended the spear further. But as Lando grabbed it, one of the Sarlacc's tentacles reached up out of the pit and and wrapped itself around Lando's leg. Han aimed a laser pistol downward and shot the winding tentacle. The Sarlacc released its tentacle and Han pulled Lando to safety.

In the meantime, Leia had done away with Jabba the Hutt and freed herself from her chains. Gathering R2 and C-3PO, she found her way to the upper deck of Jabba's barge. She was in luck. Luke had made his way across the sand and had come to rescue her.

Luke fought his way past Jabba's guards with his lightsaber. Then Leia reversed the barge's cannon so that it fired directly at the deck of the barge. Finally, Luke grabbed hold of one of the ship's rigging ropes. Gathering the beautiful princess in his arms, he swung away from the barge and back to the skiff. By the time he and Leia were safely aboard the skiff, the barge exploded, destroying Jabba and his crew.

Aboard the half-finished Death Star, thousands of Imperial troops stood in formation in the main docking bay. They waited patiently as a shuttle craft entered the enormous room and came to rest. When the shuttle's hatch opened a man emerged. The man wore a long cloak with a hood that partially hid his hideously ugly face.

The troops snapped to rigid attention. The man was the Emperor himself, the Supreme Ruler of the Galaxy.

Darth Vader knelt before the Emperor. "The Death Star will be completed on schedule," reported Vader as he rose to his feet.

"You have done well, Lord Vader," said the Emperor with a smile that showed a row of rotted teeth. "And now I sense you wish to continue your search for young Skywalker."

"Yes, my Master."

"Patience, my friend," said the Emperor. "In time he will seek you out. And when he does you must bring him before me. He has grown strong. Only together can we turn him to the dark side of the Force."

"As you wish," agreed Vader.

The Emperor smiled. "Everything is proceeding as I have foreseen," he said. Then he let out a long, evil laugh.

With Jabba the Hutt destroyed, Luke arranged to meet up with Han and the others later. Then he left Tatooine and headed straight to Dagobah. He had not forgotten his promise to Yoda. The time had come for him to finish his Jedi training.

But when he arrived on the fog-shrouded planet, he saw that his Jedi Master seemed very weak. This worried him.

"Sick I have become," admitted Yoda as he lay in bed in his tiny, mud-covered house. "Old and weak. Soon I will rest. Yes, forever sleep. Earned it, I have."

Luke was sad that Yoda was so ill. "Master Yoda," he said. "You can't die."

"That is the way of things," replied Yoda. "The way of the Force."

"But I need your help," said Luke. "I've come back to complete the training."

"No more training do you require," said Yoda. "Already you know that which you need."

"Then I am a Jedi," said Luke.

"Not yet," replied Yoda, shaking his head weakly. "You must confront Vader. Then, and only then, a Jedi will you be."

Yoda beckoned Luke closer to him. "Luke," he whispered with great effort. "There is . . . another . . . Sky . . . walker . . ."

And with that Yoda closed his eyes and disappeared into thin air forever.

Luke shivered. With Yoda gone he suddenly felt very alone. He wondered if he had the strength to resist the dark side of the Force. And how could he confront Darth Vader, his own father? And who was this other Skywalker?

"I can't do it," Luke told R2 when he returned to his spaceship. "I can't go on alone."

"Yoda will always be with you," came a familiar voice. Luke spun around. The ghostly image of Obi-Wan Kenobi had appeared behind him.

"I can't kill my own father," insisted Luke.

"Then the Emperor has already won," said Ben. "You were our only hope."

"Yoda spoke of another," said Luke.

"The other he spoke of is your twin sister," said Ben.

"But I have no sister," said Luke.

Ben explained to Luke that the identity of his sister was kept a secret to protect her from the Emperor. Then by some inner sense Luke suddenly realized who his sister was.

"Leia!" he exclaimed, stunned. "Leia is my sister!"

Luke immediately joined the Rebel Alliance at their headquarters in the largest of their star cruisers, the Headquarters Frigate, *Home One*. There, he was reunited with Han and the others. In a special meeting he learned that the Empire was building another Death Star. The unfinished Death Star was orbiting the small forest moon of Endor. A special energy shield, generated from Endor, was protecting it. Together with Han, Chewbacca, and Leia, Luke volunteered to locate and destroy the energy shield. Once the shield was destroyed, Lando Calrissian would lead a Rebel attack from the *Millennium Falcon* and destroy the Death Star.

No sooner had Luke and his team neared Endor in a stolen Imperial shuttle than a strange sensation came over him.

"Vader's on that ship," said Luke, pointing to a Star Destroyer nearby. Luke felt worried. He knew that Vader was after him. He wondered: Would his presence jeopardize the Rebel mission?

After landing undetected on Endor, Luke and the others began to search the dense forest landscape for the Empire's shield generator. No sooner had they climbed out of their ship than they caught sight of two Imperial scout troopers wandering through a valley.

"This whole party'll be for nothing if they see us," warned Han. "Chewie and I will take care of this."

Han and Chewie sneaked up behind the scouts. But one of the scouts heard them and spun around, knocking Han back. The other scout, seeing the danger, jumped onto his nearby speeder bike and took off. Chewie aimed his laser pistol and blasted the fleeing scout.

Just then Luke and Leia saw two more scouts fleeing on speeder bikes. Spotting an empty bike nearby, the two Rebels climbed onto it and sped after the Imperial troopers.

"Move closer!" Luke shouted. Leia leaned forward and gunned the bike. Soon they were right beside one of the fleeing troopers. Luke leaped onto the trooper's bike and flipped the trooper off the vehicle. Then he and Leia tore off after the remaining scout.

Now two more troopers appeared on speeder bikes. Luke went after them, leaving Leia to continue chasing the first. Leia sped after the trooper, skillfully darting around the passing trees. Finally, she pulled up alongside him. Surprised, the trooper pulled out a blaster and blasted her bike, sending it out of control. The trooper's bike then crashed.

Leia leaped off her bike just before it collided with a tree and exploded. It was the last thing she remembered before hitting the ground and passing out.

When Leia awoke, the first thing she saw was a furry face looking down at her. The face belonged to a creature who stood only about a meter tall. The creature was completely covered in fur. But this creature was no toy bear. The first thing he did was poke at her with a spear. Leia cowered, thinking the creature meant her harm.

"Cut it out!" she shouted. At the sound of her voice the creature backed off. To her surprise he even seemed a little timid. Leia smiled. "I'm not going to hurt you," she promised.

Leia could tell that she and the creature had become fast friends. When an Imperial scout trooper suddenly approached Leia from the woods, the little furry creature hid beneath a log and jabbed the scout with his spear. Then Leia hit the scout with a branch, knocking him unconscious.

"Come on," Leia said, taking the furry creature by the hand. "Let's get out of here."

Luke successfully hunted down and destroyed the two Imperial scout troopers he had been chasing. Then he rejoined Han, Chewbacca, and the droids. When Leia did not reappear, the Rebels became worried and set out to look for her. Before long they found her helmet lying near the wreckage of her speeder bike. The princess herself was nowhere to be found.

Just then Chewbacca noticed a dead animal tied to a stake in the ground. Feeling hungry, the Wookiee grabbed the creature. No sooner had he done so than a great net sprang up and scooped up the five of them. It was a trap!

"Nice work, Chewie," remarked Han as he struggled to move inside the net. "Always thinking with your stomach!"

Thinking quickly, R2 extended a small cutting blade from his hull and carefully cut away at the net. Before long the small group of Rebels found themselves falling to the ground below. But as they rose to their feet, they were suddenly surrounded by a band of small fur-creatures, each brandishing his own special weapon.

Realizing they were trapped, Han, Luke, and Chewbacca handed their weapons over to the strange forest creatures.

But when C-3PO stood up, the little creatures gasped and watched the golden droid with awe. Then they began to chant at C-3PO.

"I do believe they think I am some sort of god," C-3PO explained to the others. Not only could he understand their language, but he determined that the little creatures were called Ewoks and had lived on Endor for many centuries.

The Rebels followed the Ewoks to their village, an elaborate maze of tree houses and wood walkways. There they were reunited with Leia, who explained how she had been rescued earlier. Later, C-3PO gathered the tribe of forest dwellers around and explained that their little world of Endor was in danger of being taken over by the evil forces of the Empire. When C-3PO finished, the leader of the Ewoks stood up and pronounced the Rebels honorary members of his tribe. He then vowed to help the Rebels fight the Empire.

Afterward Luke and Leia went for a walk together. Leia could sense that something was bothering Luke.

"Luke," she said. "What's wrong?"

"Vader is here," replied Luke. "He can feel when I'm near. I have to face him."

"Why?" asked Leia.

"He's my father," admitted Luke. "If I don't make it back, you're the only hope for the Alliance."

"Don't talk that way," said Leia. "You have a power I don't understand and could never have."

"You have the power, too," Luke said. "The Force is strong in my family." He told Leia that she was his sister.

Leia smiled. "I know," she said. "Somehow, I've always known."

"Then you know why I have to face him," Luke said. "There is good in him. I've felt it. I can save him. I can turn him back to the good side. I have to try."

And with that Luke left to surrender to Darth Vader. It was the only way, he realized, that he could meet his father face to face.

"The Emperor has been expecting you," Darth Vader told Luke as soon as they were alone.

"I know, Father," said Luke.

"You are powerful, as the Emperor has foreseen," said Vader.

"Come with me," Luke pleaded. He was hoping Vader would see the evil of his ways and return to the good side of the Force.

"You don't know the power of the dark side," said Vader. "I must obey my master."

"Search your feelings, Father," said Luke. "You can't do this. I feel the conflict within you. Let go of your hate."

"It is too late for me, son," said Vader. And with that he brought Luke to the Emperor's throne room on the Death Star.

"In time you will call me 'Master,'" the Emperor told Luke.

"You're gravely mistaken," replied Luke. "You won't convert me as you did my father."

"By now you must know your father can never be turned from the dark side. So will it be with you."

"You're wrong," said Luke. "Soon I'll be dead . . . and you with me."

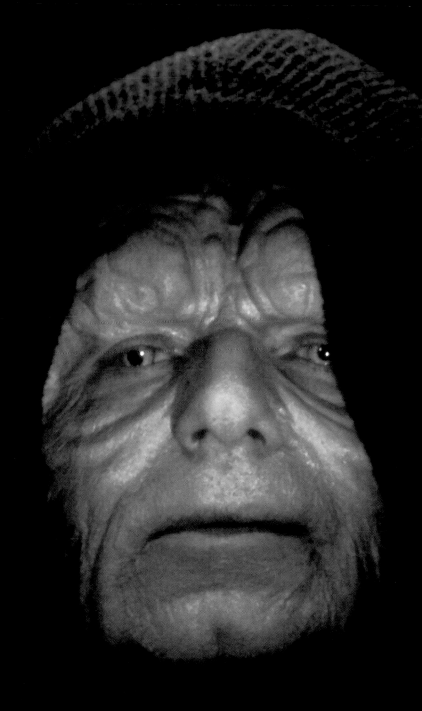

The Emperor laughed. "Perhaps you refer to the imminent attack of your Rebel fleet. Your friends are walking into a trap as is your Rebel fleet! I'm afraid the deflector shield will be quite operational when your friends arrive!"

Luke felt helpless as he looked through the viewport at the moon of Endor. In a few moments, Lando and the Rebel fleet would arrive. If what the Emperor said was true, they were doomed.

On the forest moon of Endor, Han, Leia, Chewbacca, and two Ewok guides came to a stop on a ridge that overlooked the Empire's power generator. Several Imperial troopers stood guard outside. Han and Chewie decided to sneak around the back of the generator and launch a surprise attack on the guards. Before they had time to move, however, one of the Ewoks jumped down and boarded an Imperial speeder bike.

"There goes our surprise attack," sighed Han.

But the Ewok revved up the bike and took off. All of the guards except one became alarmed and chased after him.

"Not bad for a little furball," exclaimed Han happily. Then he and the others leaped down and surprised the remaining guard, leading him to a team of Rebel reinforcements.

Han, Leia, and Chewbacca quickly entered the generator building and began planting explosives. No sooner had they started than the door opened and a team of Imperial soldiers, poised with blasters, entered the room and encircled them. The soldiers led Han and the others back outside. The generator was now surrounded by several building-size, two-legged scout walkers and hundreds of stormtroopers.

Suddenly an Ewok battle horn sounded. Then hundreds of little Ewoks, each armed with weapons, leaped out of the forest and attacked the Imperial stormtroopers.

In the confusion, Han and the others raced to the generator door. R2 tried to open the door by plugging into its computer terminal. All of a sudden a laser blast from an Imperial trooper sent R2 reeling. Lando and the Rebel fleet would be arriving any second. If Han didn't demolish the generator soon, the Rebel fleet would most certainly be destroyed.

Aboard the Death Star, Luke watched helplessly as the Rebel fleet, led by the *Millennium Falcon*, appeared out of hyperspace. Lando and the others were expecting that the Death Star's energy field would be down by now. But that was not the case. No sooner had the Rebels arrived than they were attacked by Imperial TIE fighters.

Luke could feel the anger and hatred welling up inside of him. He knew the dark side of the Force was trying to take over.

"The hate is swelling in you now," the Emperor said to Luke with a hideous laugh. "Take your Jedi weapon. Use it. Strike me down with all your hatred and your journey to the dark side will be complete!"

Luke stared at his lightsaber, which the Emperor had taken from him.

"No!" exclaimed Luke. But his anger had become too great. Outside, the Rebels were losing. He could resist no longer. He grabbed his lightsaber and ignited it, instantly taking a swing at the Emperor. But before his sword could reach the ugly monarch, Darth Vader's lightsaber blocked the blow.

Luke now turned to fight his father. The two Skywalkers lunged at each other, each parrying the other's blows. To his surprise Luke found it wasn't difficult to knock Vader off balance. It was obvious, as Vader tumbled down a flight of stairs, that Luke had become a powerful Jedi.

"Good!" said Vader. "Let the hate flow through you."

Luke realized that the dark side of the Force was beginning to affect him. He turned off his lightsaber and drove the hate from his being.

"I will not fight you, Father," Luke said gently. "I feel the good in you."

But now Vader climbed back upstairs, attacking Luke.

"You couldn't bring yourself to kill me before," Luke reminded Vader as he darted away from his father's lightsaber, "and I don't believe you'll destroy me now."

Just then Vader stopped and Luke knew that the evil lord had sensed something.

"Sister!" said Vader. He sensed Luke's loyalty to Leia. "So, you have a twin sister. If you will not turn to the dark side, then perhaps she will."

"Never!" exclaimed Luke, angrily. He ignited his lightsaber and attacked Vader with all his strength, finally driving his father to the floor.

"Good!" laughed the Emperor, who had been watching the entire fight with evil glee. "Your hate has made you powerful. Now, fulfill your destiny and take your father's place at my side!"

Luke hesitated. He realized how angry he had become. He had been swayed by the dark side.

"Never!" he exclaimed, hurling his lightsaber away triumphantly.

"So be it, Jedi," said the Emperor. And with that the Emperor pointed his arms at Luke and let out a series of powerful electric bolts. Luke went flying to the ground, weakened almost to the point of death.

"Father," Luke groaned, calling out to Vader. "Please help me..."

Vader stood up and watched as the Emperor sent another blast of electricity into Luke's helpless body.

"Now, young Skywalker," the Emperor said. "You will die!"

Han had opened the computer panel to the generator bunker and had begun to cross the wires in the hopes of opening the door. Meanwhile Leia kept him covered by blasting away at any oncoming stormtroopers. Suddenly she took a laser blast to her shoulder and fell against the wall.

"Freeze!" exclaimed the stormtrooper who had come upon them. "Don't move!"

Han froze. Then he looked down. Leia, who was partially hidden behind a wall, had her laser pointed right at the stormtrooper.

"I love you," Han told her quietly as they silently acknowledged a plan.

"I know," said Leia. Then Han slowly stepped aside. Leia fired, knocking the stormtrooper to the ground. Just as Han leaned over to help Leia to her feet, he looked up to see a giant scout walker approach, its deadly weapons aimed right at them. Helpless, Han froze again. But when the walker's hatch popped up, Chewie rose out through the opening. The Wookiee had commandeered the chicken-like walker from the Imperial troopers.

Thinking quickly, Han climbed into the walker, put on a trooper's helmet and contacted the Imperial commander inside the generator bunker. It worked. He fooled the commander into thinking he was an Imperial trooper who needed extra soldiers to help fight the Rebels. The commander sent his soldiers out to help. Outside Han and the others surprised the troops and disarmed them.

Within minutes Han, Leia, and Chewbacca raided the generator control room. Then they began to plant the explosives that would destroy the generator and the energy shield that protected the Death Star from attack.

Luke writhed in pain as the Emperor blasted him again and again with bolts of deadly electricity. He looked helplessly up from the floor of the Emperor's chamber and once again begged Vader for help.

Vader looked at Luke. Then he looked at the Emperor.

Luke wasn't sure, but he thought he felt the dark side of the force weakening inside his father. Suddenly Vader grabbed the Emperor from behind and lifted him above his head.

But the Emperor fought back, sending charge after charge of electricity into Vader's body. Vader was growing weak, but with a sudden surge of strength he sent the Emperor flying over a railing and deep into the central power core of the Death Star.

No sooner had the Emperor been destroyed than Vader collapsed on the floor. Luke rushed to his father's side.

"Luke," Vader whispered weakly. "Help me take this mask off."

"But you'll die," said Luke.

"Nothing can stop that now," replied his father. "Just for once let me look on you with my own eyes."

Slowly, Luke removed the mask from Vader's face. Beneath the mask was the heavily scarred face of an elderly man, a man once known as Anakin Skywalker.

"Now, go, my son," said Luke's father. "Leave me."

"No," said Luke, tears welling in his eyes. "You're coming with me. I can't leave you here. I've got to save you."

"You already have, Luke," his father said, just before passing away.

Although his father was gone, Luke smiled. He knew the dark side had been driven away from his father. Darth Vader was gone.

Just then Luke felt an explosion rock the Death Star. Glancing up through the viewport he saw that Lando and the Rebels were now blasting the Imperial battle station with their torpedoes. Half carrying, half dragging his father's body, he made his way to a shuttle and blasted off.

From the shuttle, Luke watched as Lando, piloting the *Millennium Falcon*, led the final charge into the Death Star. A chain of explosions went off through the battle station. The structure began to collapse, but the *Millennium Falcon* was nowhere to be seen. Had something gone wrong?

47

Just as the docking bay section of the station exploded, the *Millennium Falcon* rocketed away from the Death Star. Then in one final, spectacular blast, the Death Star exploded.

The Rebels had won. At long last the Empire had been defeated.

That evening a victory celebration took place on the moon of Endor. The Ewoks cooked a great feast and everyone danced to happy music. When Luke arrived he was greeted with hugs from Leia, Han, and Chewbacca. As the party progressed Luke felt his thoughts drifting elsewhere. All at once he felt the Force inside him. He looked into the distance. There, he could see the smiling, shimmering figures of Obi-Wan Kenobi and Yoda. There was a third person with them as well. It was Luke's father, Anakin Skywalker, now reunited with them on the light side of the Force.

And he was smiling, too.

THE END